Carlos, Light the Farolito

By **Jean Ciavonne**

Illustrated by **Donna Clair**

Clarion Books/New York

Clarion Books
a Houghton Mifflin Company imprint
215 Park Avenue South, New York, NY 10003
Text copyright © 1995 by the Estate of Jean Ciavonne
Illustrations copyright © 1995 by Donna Clair

The illustrations for this book were executed in acrylics.
The text was set in 15/18.5-point Cantoria.

Printed in the USA

Library of Congress Cataloging-in-Publication Data

Ciavonne, Jean.
Carlos, light the farolito / by Jean Ciavonne ; illustrated by Donna Clair.
p. ; cm.
Summary: When his parents and grandfather are late on Christmas Eve,
it's up to Carlos to take over his grandfather's role in the traditional Mexican
reenactment of the Nativity called Las Posadas.
ISBN 0-395-66759-3
[1. Posadas (Social custom)—Fiction.   2. Mexican Americans—Fiction.
3. Christmas—Fiction.]   I. Clair, Donna, ill.   II. Title.
PZ7.C4905Car   1995
[E]—dc20   94-24510
CIP
AC

WOZ 10 9 8 7 6 5 4 3 2 1

E
FICTION
CIA

To Dorothy Ostrom Worrell, who gave me a *farolito*, and who wrote a newspaper column about *Las Posadas* that brought warm memories of Spanish-speaking children I taught. To Jane Fitz-Randolph and to my husband Michael for having faith in my story. To my grandchildren, Allegra, Patrick, Luke, Adriane, and Dominic, with the hope that they will feel the joy of Christmas that Carlos knows.

—J.C.

Para mi amigito Isaac Gonzales.

—D.C.

Carlos Castillo knelt before the little crèche in the living room. Angels surrounded Joseph, Mary, and the Baby, the shepherds and animals. Carlos admired the small, brightly colored clay figures.

Delightful fragrances drifted in from the kitchen, the strong spicy smells of tamales and empanadas stuffed with meat, and the cinnamony aroma of *bunuelos,* little fried pies filled with sweetened fruit. Carlos's mother and aunt had baked for days, and Aunt Romelia was still in the kitchen, making sure there would be enough food.

1

For tonight the *peregrinos* would come to the Castillo home to celebrate the ninth and last night of *Las Posadas,* "the lodgings." Nine families, all friends and neighbors, would be the *peregrinos,* wanderers in search of shelter for Mary and Joseph. And Carlos's grandfather always sang the role of the innkeeper. It was an honor to host the final night of *Las Posadas,* and Carlos was sure his home had been chosen because of Grandfather's big, booming voice, as well as the wonderful food Mama and Aunt Romelia always prepared.

Carlos lifted the Baby out of the tiny manger, gave Him a kiss, and gently returned Him to His place in the *Nacimiento.*

The mouthwatering smells were making Carlos hungry. He got up and ran to the kitchen. "Aunt Romelia, may I please have a taste of something?" Carlos begged his aunt.

Aunt Romelia turned from the stove, smiling. "One *biscochito,*" she said.

"When will Mama and Papa be back?" Carlos asked, munching the spicy cookie. Carlos's parents and his grandfather had gone to the city to buy goodies to fill the piñata for the party.

"Soon," said Aunt Romelia. "Don't worry, they'll be here in plenty of time. Come, let's take these trays out to the patio."

Carlos put his tray down on the long lace-covered table, near one of the tall candlesticks. The piñata that Papa had made was already hanging from a sturdy tree. It was a shaggy donkey, like the one that had carried Mary, the mother of Jesus, to Bethlehem.

"Let's use these pretty napkins to cover the food until our guests come," said Aunt Romelia.

"I can't wait until *Las Posadas*!" said Carlos, carefully placing a napkin over neat rows of golden pastries. "Tonight is my favorite night of the whole year. Except . . ."

"Except what, Carlos?" Aunt Romelia prompted gently.

"Except staying home with Señora Abeyta from next door while you and Mama and Papa and Grandfather go to the *Misa del Gallo*."

Some people said the midnight mass on Christmas Eve took its name—the Mass of the Rooster—from the lateness of the hour. Others said it was because the *gallo* was the first creature to announce the holy birth. Carlos wished he, too, were going tonight to see the life-size *Nacimiento* at the Cathedral, lit with glowing candles.

"You'll come with us when you're older," Aunt Romelia assured him. "I know, it's hard to wait." She bustled toward the kitchen.

Carlos saw that evening shadows were creeping over the patio. Why didn't his parents come home?

Maybe they were driving up now. Carlos stepped inside and hurried to the front window. But the street was empty. He wandered from the living room to the kitchen to the patio and back to the living room again. Would the afternoon ever end? Yet he didn't want night to arrive before his family did.

From the front window Carlos saw a *farol* shining above the door of the house across the way. As he watched, another *farol* twinkled into light, and another. Soon these lanterns of glass and tin would gleam at every doorway in the neighborhood, just as they had for the past eight nights, to light the way for the Christ Child in case he should return to earth seeking shelter.

"Aunt Romelia!" Carlos called. "It's time for our *farolito*!" As she entered the room, he added, "Please may I light the candle?"

His aunt nodded and took a long fireplace match from the mantel. Together they went outside. Carlos reached up and opened the little door of the lantern. Aunt Romelia struck the match, handed it to Carlos, and watched as he lit the candle inside the lantern.

Now it was time for a silent prayer. Carlos bowed his head. He prayed that the *faroles* all along the rows of houses would light the Christ Child's way tonight. And that Mama, Papa, and Grandfather would arrive home safely and soon. Very soon. He raised his eyes to his *farol,* glowing bravely in the dusk.

8

The telephone rang, and Carlos raced to answer it. What a relief it was to hear Grandfather's voice! "After we bought the favors and candy for the piñata, the car broke down, *hijito*," Grandfather told him. "We had it repaired, and now we're coming home. Perhaps you and Aunt Romelia should light our *farolito*."

"It's already lit, Grandfather."

"Good. *Hasta la vista,* Carlos. We'll be home soon."

As Carlos laid the phone down, he heard faintly from outside a plaintive melody. His heart sank. Oh, no. Not yet! But the music grew louder. Carlos ran to the front window, his heart pounding. It was the *Las Posadas* procession!

Children led the way carrying *andas,* small statues of Mary and Joseph, on a platform of evergreen branches. Behind them, swinging lanterns, came the adult *peregrinos,* two by two. They were turning up the walk to the Castillo home.

Quickly Carlos and Aunt Romelia turned off all the
lights in the house until only the *farol* was shining. That
was the custom. Carlos crouched behind the door. A big,
hard lump formed in his chest.

The *peregrinos* outside sang their weary song, verses
hundreds of years old:

> "We have come a long journey
> And are asking a place to rest."

At the sound of the familiar words, a shiver ran down
Carlos's back.

Now the *peregrinos* were knocking. The man representing
Joseph called for lodgings for his beloved wife, who could
go no farther:

> "In the name of heaven
> I ask shelter for us."

Time for Grandfather to thunder out the words of the hard-hearted innkeeper! In other years, when Grandfather shouted to the *peregrinos* to go away before they awakened the guests at the inn, Carlos himself trembled. But Grandfather was not here. And the *peregrinos* stood outside waiting for the innkeeper's answer.

The great icy lump in Carlos's chest felt like a stone. His heart thumped loud and fast. He looked at Aunt Romelia. "What'll we do now?" he whispered.

"You must sing the words of the innkeeper, Carlos," his aunt said softly.

Carlos gasped. "Oh, no. I can't! You sing them, Aunt." He felt his lips quiver.

"No," his aunt said. "The innkeeper is a man. A man should sing those words. You must take Grandfather's place."

Of course Carlos knew the words of the innkeeper. Hadn't he heard them every Christmas of his life? But sing them now, for *Las Posadas*? He could scarcely breathe.

The *peregrinos* were surely wondering why Grandfather didn't sing out. Joseph knocked again and repeated his plea: "In the name of heaven . . ."

Aunt Romelia put her hands on Carlos's shoulders. "You can do it, Carlos. Sing."

Carlos sighed. He swallowed. Then he lifted his chin and began to sing in a quavery voice so soft he himself could barely hear the words. "Go away!" he sang.

"Louder. They can't hear you through the door. A little louder." Aunt Romelia patted his shoulder encouragingly.

Carlos drew a long shuddering breath and forced himself to sing louder:

"Go away. I cannot open the door."

Joseph pleaded again for entrance:
        "I am a carpenter from Nazareth.
        My name is Joseph."
Wishing his voice would stop shaking, Carlos answered:
        "I don't care who you are.
        Just let me sleep."
    Ah, it worked! Through the window Carlos watched the
peregrinos turn slowly away.

They circled the yard and knocked and pleaded again. Eight times they circled the yard. Eight times they begged to enter.

Each time Carlos sang out his refusal, his voice grew stronger. Louder. More like Grandfather's. Carlos was starting to enjoy singing those harsh words, and yet he wished he didn't have to send the *peregrinos* away. Why had that innkeeper been so mean those many years ago?

When Joseph knocked for the ninth time, the innkeeper realized the Queen of Heaven was waiting outside. Carlos shouted loudly and clearly:

"Come in, blessed Mary and good Joseph.
We welcome you with joy."

Now Carlos flung the door wide and shouted, "Come in! Come in, everyone!" As Aunt Romelia hurried to turn on all the lights, the guests entered, smiling happily but not speaking.

Everyone knelt before the *Nacimiento.* The man who had sung Joseph's words began to sing— *"Noche de paz, noche de amor"*—and the others joined in. Carlos had done his part, and now his head was spinning with joy. He let his voice soar along with Joseph's deep tones and Aunt Romelia's lilting notes. He remembered to sing the last verse softly, like a lullaby for the Baby.

Suddenly the front door burst open, and here were Mama, Papa, and Grandfather, greeting their friends with hugs and handshakes. "Excuse us, we must finish the preparations," said Papa, and he and Mama carried their packages out to the patio.

Grandfather placed a hand on Carlos's head and said to the guests, "I am sorry we were late."

"No apologies are needed, Señor Castillo," said Joseph, who was Señor Martinez from the next street. "Everything went well. Of course, the innkeeper had a higher voice than in other years."

"And a sweeter voice," his wife said, smiling at Carlos.

"Thank you, señora," Carlos said. He heard his mother calling him and ran to the patio.

Mama had turned on the lights, and Aunt Romelia was bringing in steaming, fragrant pots of coffee and cinnamon-flavored hot chocolate. Papa had just finished filling the piñata.

Mama gave Carlos a big kiss. "I'm so happy to see you, Carlos! Sorry we were so late, but you managed beautifully without us," she said. "Now go invite our guests to the patio."

The children raced to the patio. Carlos's friend Pedro got there first. He grinned while Grandfather tied a clean handkerchief over his eyes, twirled him around, and placed a stick in his hand. As Pedro swung at the piñata, Papa pulled the rope to make it fly out of reach. The children screamed with laughter.

Each child took a turn with the stick while Papa made the donkey dance to one side, then the other, now up, now down. At last the smallest girl was allowed to break it. Showers of candy, gum, small straw toys, and shiny tin whistles clattered across the tiled floor, and the children scrambled for them.

Then everyone sat down for the feast. Sitting with his friends at one end of the long table, Carlos ate until he couldn't hold another morsel.

It was growing late. Some of the smallest children had fallen asleep. Parents began gathering their families together and talking about leaving.

Grandfather came over to where Carlos was sitting. "I am proud of you, Carlos," he said gently, "for taking part in *Las Posadas.* You were very brave."

"When the *peregrinos* came and you weren't here to sing the words of the innkeeper, I was frightened," Carlos admitted. "But I tried to sing them well."

"And so you did. Next year we will sing them together." Grandfather put his hand on Carlos's shoulder. "Come along, *hijito.*"

Carlos didn't want this wonderful day to end. "Can't I stay up just a little longer, Grandfather?"

Grandfather was beaming. "Of course you can. A boy who sings the part of the innkeeper is old enough to come to midnight mass."

At first Carlos couldn't believe his ears, but there were Mama and Aunt Romelia, hugging him. Papa lifted him up high and then set him down. Carlos could not stop smiling. His heart sang.

And he marched joyfully in the procession to the Cathedral to celebrate the birth of Jesus at the hour when He was born.

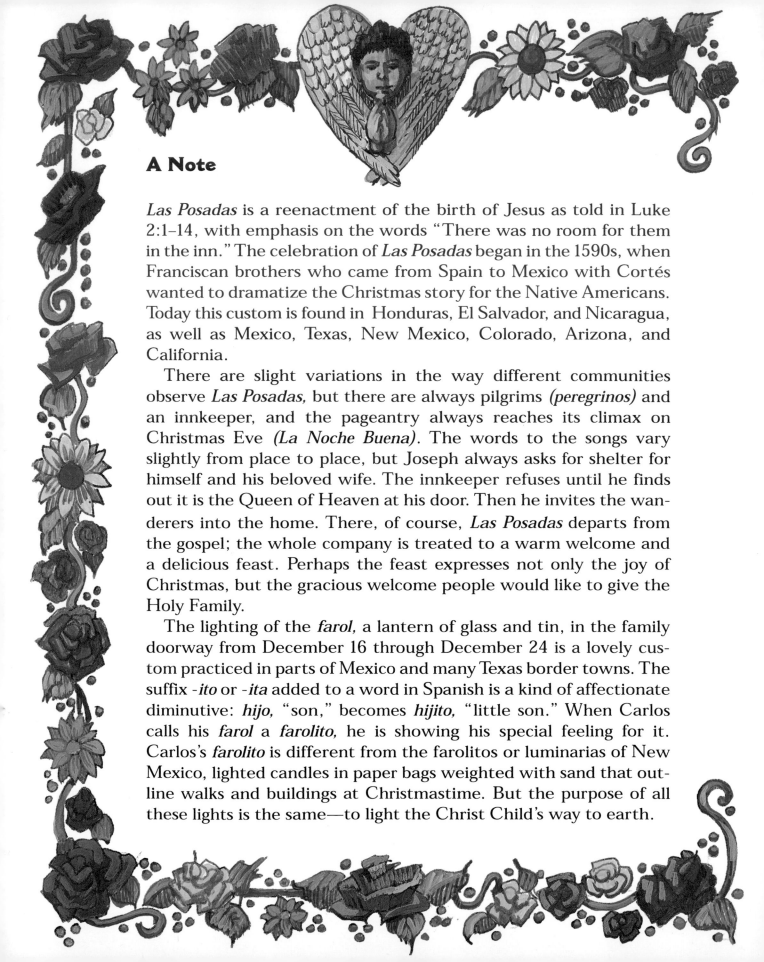

A Note

Las Posadas is a reenactment of the birth of Jesus as told in Luke 2:1–14, with emphasis on the words "There was no room for them in the inn." The celebration of *Las Posadas* began in the 1590s, when Franciscan brothers who came from Spain to Mexico with Cortés wanted to dramatize the Christmas story for the Native Americans. Today this custom is found in Honduras, El Salvador, and Nicaragua, as well as Mexico, Texas, New Mexico, Colorado, Arizona, and California.

There are slight variations in the way different communities observe *Las Posadas,* but there are always pilgrims *(peregrinos)* and an innkeeper, and the pageantry always reaches its climax on Christmas Eve *(La Noche Buena)*. The words to the songs vary slightly from place to place, but Joseph always asks for shelter for himself and his beloved wife. The innkeeper refuses until he finds out it is the Queen of Heaven at his door. Then he invites the wanderers into the home. There, of course, *Las Posadas* departs from the gospel; the whole company is treated to a warm welcome and a delicious feast. Perhaps the feast expresses not only the joy of Christmas, but the gracious welcome people would like to give the Holy Family.

The lighting of the *farol,* a lantern of glass and tin, in the family doorway from December 16 through December 24 is a lovely custom practiced in parts of Mexico and many Texas border towns. The suffix *-ito* or *-ita* added to a word in Spanish is a kind of affectionate diminutive: *hijo,* "son," becomes *hijito,* "little son." When Carlos calls his *farol* a *farolito,* he is showing his special feeling for it. Carlos's *farolito* is different from the farolitos or luminarias of New Mexico, lighted candles in paper bags weighted with sand that outline walks and buildings at Christmastime. But the purpose of all these lights is the same—to light the Christ Child's way to earth.